KARAMBOO
An African Love Story

S.K.POTTEKAT

Sankarankutty was born in Kozhikode city on 14.3.1913. His family name was Pottekkat. He wrote under the name of S.K.Pottekkat. His father, Kunjiraman was a teacher in an English high school. After finishing his education at the Ganapathi School and in the Samoothiri College without gradu-ating to a degree, he worked for three years as a teacher. In 1940 he undertook an extensive tour of India. From 1945 he became what may be called a full time traveler. He visited Africa, Europe, Sri Lanka, and Indonesia. Concurrently he took to wrintg. As a member of the Indian Delegation he visited Helsinki where the International Peace Conference was held and traveled in the Soviet Union, Czechoslovakia and Germany. In 1965 became a member of the Indian Parliament.'

He started writing with a short story named Rajaneethi which was published in the Samoothiri College Magazine. This was followed by a large number of novels of which The Story of a street' and The legend of the land' are the most famous. Travelogues form a significant part of his literary work. No other Malayalam writer has written so many arti-cles and stories on travel. The story of a street won the state Sahitya Akademi award and the legend of the land, the National Sahitya Akademy award.In 1980 the Jnan Peeth Award, the highest literary honor in India was conferred on him. He passed away on the 6th of August 1982.

KARAMBOO
An African Love Story

S.K. Pottekat

Translated by

Dr. K.Parameswaran

LIPI PUBLICATIONS
Kozhikode, Kerala, India

English

KARAMBOO:
An African Love Story

by
S.K. POTTEKKATTU

Translated by
Dr. K. Parameswaran

First Edition: September 2020

Typeset & Layout by Jaisal Nallalam
Cover Design: Firoz Padikkal

Publishers
LIPI PUBLICATIONS
Head Office
AL Ameen Building, 13/766- U 6
Rly.Stn. Link Road, Kozhikode - 673 002
Tel: 0495-2700321

Showroom
LIPI BOOKS
B-12, Vikas Building, Rly. Stn. Link Road, Kozhikode-2
Tel: 0495-2700192 Mobile: 9847262583
Email: lipipublicationsclt@gmail.com
lipiakbar@gmail.com
www.lipipublications.com

DR. K. PARAMESWARAN

(Translator)

I am Dr. K. Parameswaran, at present working as Deputy Director (News), All India Radio, Trichy, Tamil Nadu. As an Indian Information Service Officer, I have served in the publicity wing of the Union Ministry of Finance, as Field Publicity Officer in Kannur and Kovai and as Correspondant for All India Radio in Kozhikode and Thiruvananthapuram.

I hold a Master's Degree in Applied Linguistic and my Phd thesis, granted by the University of Kerala in 2007 is the one "Discourse of Radio News, with Reference to Malayalam News".

My publication includes many articles, wich are sited at the cutting edge intersection between Lingustics, Litrature and Journalism, in my mother tongue Malayalam as well as in English.

I have also published a translation into English, of the short stories by the world renowned Malayalam literature S.K Pottekkat. These stories, depicted against exotic backgrounds like Africa, Switzarland and England, have been translated into English for the first time.

An adaption of my Phd thesis has been published in English. A third book, on the history of Railways in kerala has been broght out in Malayalam recently. It was formally released by Dr Shashi Tharoor, MP in Trivandrum.

Born on 16.10.1960. I was brought up in the two Kerala cities of Kottayam and Kozhikode. My family includes wife, an electrical engineer and daughter, an advertising proffossional. My areas of interest include Astrology, Carnatic Music, Cross Words and Sanskrit Slokas.

CONTENTS

IN THE SHADOW OF AN OLD FORT

The memory of that night in the ancient port city of Mombasa in East Africa can never be erased from my mind.

I feel metamorphosing into a ghost myself, when I think about those three hours that I had spent in that land of "black men". Just imagine that you had fallen asleep in some corner of a place that is not in the least familiar to you! What will be your feelings when you realize, after having seen a sweet dream, that the place you had fallen asleep was a dilapidated cemetery? My experience had been something similar. Unknowingly falling asleep in the embrace of sheer danger; later waking up and thinking back about it – it is something more painful than actually falling into danger!

Before embarking on that story, here are a few snippets of the setting- the city, Mombasa...

It is an ancient port town wherein could be seen black people, black Arabs, a few white Arabs, Indians and a handful of Europeans! The city seems as if it was a scene that had arisen into life from an Arabian fantasy! Some forms, clad in black burquas, could be seen flitting around street corners; suddenly you may have a doubt whether you had seen them at all! Narrow roads that were slowly crumbling into nothingness! There is not the bustle and din of a busy town; only bunches of shadows – the products of the illicit relationship between darkness and moonlight –could be discerned here and there. Even the cypress trees that border the avenues seem as if they were wearing masks!

People of the city also wear masks; the only thing is that you can't see them. That Arab, wearing a white turban – he could be a spy of a pirate gang! That lean person, wearing a long, flowing dress could be an Abyssinian magician! (In the hidden recesses of his robe could perhaps be found his magic wand, fashioned out of the dried genital of a bull!) The hunch back there, seemingly a dock worker, could easily be another sorcerer. (Underneath his lengthened finger nails could be hidden the minutest blob of potent poison!) For a fee of a mere five shillings, he would be ready to kill anyone with that dosage!

From another remote corner could be heard the beat of the village drums. It seemed like the rumblings of an ogre; it had all the characteristics of an ancient, secret ritual. The beats eerily echoed the dance movements of black men in trance. They are the heartbeats of dark Africa; they attract us as well as fill us with dread – at the same time!

In the bay of Mombasa could be seen dhows ready to venture out into the deep seas. These Arab dhows carry the traditions of three thousand years of trade relations. The small islands near the coasts of East Africa had long been annexed by the Arabs of Oman. There was a time when the Portugese had made an attempt to wrest these islands for themselves. But the Arabs had defeated them and had established their rule here. At present (i.e. when the story unfolds) even though the administration of Mombasa was under the British Queen, the port city was actually the property of the Zanzibar Sultans. An yearly payment of 16,000 sovereigns was being made by the British to the Zanzibar Sultan for the control of Mombasa.

It was a moonlit night. I was standing in front of the ancient Fort Jesus of the Portugese. I am not sure how I had reached there. No one had directed me to the port. I had just come out for an evening walk. I had crisscrossed the labyrinth of old streets in the ancient part of the city, wandering with utter disregard whatsoever to time and place, had meandered around the city, and had finally reached here in front of the dilapidated fort! That's all that could be said!

At times I had a fleeting feeling whether constant touch with the sounds and smells of the African culture had engendered some demonic change in me too! But I was in no way frightened. Rather I felt like a small boy, let loose in the premises of the vast museum of African culture! The feelings uppermost in my mind were a child like curiosity, tinged with the excitement of expectancy!

In the forefront of Fort Jesus could be found a lawn, bordered with various types of flowering trees. On one side of the lawn one could espy an old verandah, inlaid with stones. I sat on the verandah in a yogic pose and looked over the fort. In the moonlight, the fort resembled a huge cemetery!

In fact, the Fort Jesus was indeed a cemetery – a cemetery

devoted to history! It was a memorial to the attacks, mass killings and betrayals made by the Portugese in East Africa.

The church, which had been built by a Baptist named John, in the holy name of Jesus, later became the venue for the dance of the devil in the ensuing centuries. The number of corpses that were collected from the fort easily outnumbered the number of bricks used to build up the fort! Streams of blood have flown on its floors! Soldiers- tired, unwell, weary and hungry- had to take recourse to eating human meat, like veritable ghosts, in the interiors of this very fort! People who were in the know of the history of the fort never dared to come near it.

One part of the fort was being made use of by the British as a jail. The Portugese had originally constructed this fort as a base from which to thwart the attacks of the Oman Arabs, their principal allies in the African sub continent. They had tried the technique of influencing local rulers, making them fight against each other and capture the power in the midst of all these confusions. Thus they saw to it that Hassan Bin Ali, the Muslim King of Malindi was appointed as the ruler of Mombasa. When he realized that the actual powers were being wielded by the head of the Portugese soldiers in the fort, Hasan Ali began to oppose him. But realizing this to be futile, he later ran away to the African jungles and sought asylum with the Rabai tribe. But the Portugese prevailed upon a gang of Rabai tribesmen to get Hasan Ali killed.

Then their attention turned to Hassan Ali's sun Yoosuf. They realized that if things can be handled by a loyal local leader, the expenses of maintaining a Portugese army in the African nation can be considerably brought down. They also intelligently realized that the common man was more likely to listen to the orders of a local leader. With these intentions in mind, the Portugese government decided to send Yoosuf to Goa for higher studies. During his absence, Mombasa continued to be ruled by the Portugese.

But things developed in another direction. Yoosuf fell in love with a Portugese girl. He converted into Roman Catholicism in order to marry this girl. Yoosuf took the name of Joseph and returned to Mombasa in 1630 and demanded back his kingship. Foreign life, modern education, marriage and conversion did nothing to reduce the potency of Arab blood that ran through Yoosuf's veins. The Portugese were not ready to return the throne of Mombasa to Yoosuf. The group of Arabs who came to the Jesus Fort to argue for Yoosuf was massacred by the Portugese. Following this a bloody fight transpired between the Arabs and the Portugese. Realizing that it won't be possible to stand up to the Portugese, Yoosuf also ran away to Arabia. Just like his father Yoosuf was also beheaded by a gang, which was paid handsomely by the Portugese.

Thus the fort in front of which I am standing was a mute witness to many a bloodshed and dramatic developments.

The historical significance of the fort doesn't end there. The longest war, in the entire history of Mombasa, began thirty long years after the murder of Yoosuf. In the year 1696, the then Oman sultan Saif embarked upon a determined campaign to drive out the Portugese from Mombasa for all time! His well equipped army landed on the Mombasa port, annexed the city and opened an all out attack on Fort Jesus. There were less than 50 Europeans in the fort at that time. A motley crowd of about 2000, consisting of converted Christians and their families, had also sought asylum in the fort.

The siege on the fort lasted a record two years and nine months. The Oman army had planned to make the people inside the fort starve to death by effectively casting an embargo on the movement of men and materials into the fort. The plan proved effective. Even as the Oman soldiers celebrated their victory with dance, music and feasts outside the Jesus fort, the motley crowd inside the fort slowly starved themselves to death.

I sat on the verandah, thinking about that historical siege of the Momabasa Fort Jesus. The fort could be seen more clearly in the glistening moon light. The shadows lurking on the sides of the daunting fort attained increased density as the night progressed. A warm breeze coming from the sea embraced me. I sat looking at the fort with unblinking eyes. This was the soil on which 2000 innocent people fell dead inch by inch – literally! The ghosts of Europeans, black aboriginals, converted Christians as well as African natives might still be lurking in the environs of the fort. I felt as if I could see the final episodes of heir lives – sans ointments for their wounds, sans water to drink, their lives ebbing out falling prey to diseases…

Suddenly I espied a shadow coming towards me – it seemed that of a human. I felt slightly apprehensive. I thought that the form had suddenly materialized out of air. I peered at the form closely. That form too seemed to be examining me carefully from the shadows of the walled court. He might have been able to see me much better because of the moonlight falling on my face.

The status quo lasted, may be a few minutes! Then the form moved forward towards me, towards the moon light. It turned out to be a well dressed Arab, a red Turkish fez adding color to his attire.

I gave him a hint of a friendly smile, but could discern no change on his face. He stood his stance, staring at me with some intensity! I smiled yet again.

At that he asked me something in the native Swahili language. I was least conversant in Swahili. I gestured that I did not understand what he had said. I also told him in English that I didn't know Swahili.

Then he started speaking in English. It was evident that he had no formal education. His butler English bore all the signs of having been learned from listening to the servant's in a European's house hold.

"How long have you been sitting here?" - was his next question. "It might be about half an hour" – I replied calmly.

"Did anyone come here? A, a woman dressed in a burqua…?"

"No, I didn't see anyone", was my reply.

He stood, thinking over something, looked around and then slowly walked around and sat beside me.

I looked over him closely. He was middle aged, with a curved nose line and a sharp chin. He was one eyed – a glittering eye that shown in the moonlight.

"Where is your shop?" was his next question. He automatically had come to the conclusion that I was an Indian merchant.

I assured him that I was not a trader and that I was traveler. "Oh, you have come to see Mombasa! Have you seen the whole of

Mombasa?"

"No", replied I. "it is just two days since I reached here". "Where are you staying?" was his next question. I told him and was rewarded with a few minutes of silence.

"Why have you come to this corner of the fort?" The question came out unexpectedly, in quite a strained voice. I felt that the Arab was accusing me of doing something wrong. His sole eye shone threateningly like a bejeweled dagger head.

"I had come out on an evening walk and by chance, landed up here; that is all", I replied smilingly.

"What is so attractive to you in this Godforsaken corner, let me see!" I could understand that there was some ulterior motive behind this line of questioning. I spoke out – "here, I was thinking about that fort. Its history, the long siege that took place more than two centuries back...etc!"

On hearing this, the Arab's face brightened. He smiled. "Oh! You have heard all these stories?" "I too have read some history books" – I replied. "It is not enough to know about this partially. It is a story that you should know in all its detail". To this I responded that I was all agog to hear the whole story.

Remembering something, he suddenly he asked "what is the time?"

I replied that I didn't have a watch. And at that exact moment the clock tower of the fort started ring out the hour! I counted – 1,2,3,4,5,6,7,8,9.

I could see his face changing with the clanging of the clock!

The clock had only struck four times, when he covered his ears, as if he could bear no more.

Later he removed his hand, and asked with annoyance "what is the time?" "It's past nine" I replied.

I felt sad for that man who was affected by the sound of tolling bells. "Why are you affected badly by the ringing of the clock?", I asked him sympathetically.

He didn't seem to hear the question. A little while later, he said to him self "I have to go to see a cinema at 9.30."

Who is this Arab? I remembered that he hadn't introduced himself. If he is not ready to introduce himself, I may as well ask him. "Hey, you have not said anything about yourself. What is your name?"

He didn't reply immediately. After a few seconds his reply came out in a booming voice "Hassan Bin Ali"!

◆

THE SMILE OF A RING

Hassan Bin Ali! I repeated the name of that Arab once or twice in my mind. It was the very same name of the King of Milind, who had been elevated as the King of Mombasa 350 years ago by the Portugese and later killed by them.

I offered Hassan a cigarette. He shook his head and said "I don't smoke". I lighted up a cigarette and asked him: "Mr Hassan, what are you doing in Mombasa?" There was no immediate reply. A minute later he said" I am an agent who supplies food materials to ships." What business did a food and catering agent had in this lonely corner of the fort, was the question that immediately came to my mind. But that question went unspoken.

The initial roughness evident in Hassan's face slowly started receding. His apprehensiveness and anxiety slowly melted away. He began to sing an Arab song. I had been attracted to Arabian music right from the first time I had heard it. Even though I couldn't understand the meanings of the lyrics, the power of the music invariable engendered an unexplainable sense of excitement in me. The soft syllables of the Arabian music, which originated from the depths of the heart and pulsated out through the throat and lips of the singer, had a magical quality of attractiveness.

"Ha... what a sweet song", I congratulated Hassan. He shut his only eye, shook his head and graciously accepted my appreciation with a soft smile. "Mr Hassan, could you please tell me the meaning of those lyrics?" Hassan's only eye seemed to reflect an unexpected feeling of shyness, as if full of the dregs of an old romance! He smiled suggestively and said "It is a love song and it means thus:

In Sanzibar doth the perfume laden wind circulate at dusk,

And young minds run hither and thither, afflicted by the perfumes of love!

The flute beckons in Sanzibar, nectar oozes in its coastal regions,

Ha, doth the whole of East Africa dance with abandon!"

When I remarked that the meaning of the song far overtakes the beauty of its music, Hassan repeated it for me once again. He said "Sanzibar is a land that reverberates with the perfume of cloves, the laughter of black beauties and the sweetness of love songs. I belong to Sanzibar!"

I was excited. "Oh, you are an islander from Sanzibar" I exclaimed. "Yes! I am a Shirazi" he replied.

A short spell of silence followed. Then, shutting his only eye once again, giving a lopsided smile that hinted at mischievousness, the Shirazi whispered in my ears "there are two things that I love the most!" "What are they?" I asked, my eyes rounded with excitement. He replied "one, love songs"... a pause again. Hassan watched me meaningfully, his eye gleaming! I couldn't wait. I asked "The other?"

"Murder", he droned in my ears!

I laughed out aloud. I understood that Hassan was speaking about films and cinema. I also remembered that the Roxy cinema theatre in Mombasa was showing a film titled "Murderer" at that time. I responded "I don't like films full of fighting and murders. I like romantic love stories".

Hassan did not respond. He kept looking this way and that, a trifle worried and anxious. After a while he asked "Oh, you like love stories, isn't it?" "Yes. I must say that the love stories in the famous Thousand and One Nights attract me more than the black beauties of Sanzibar" – I replied.

"Do you know that this very Fort Jesus had been the setting for a marvelous love story?" Hassan asked me. "No. I have heard only stories of mass killings that had taken place in the fort." "The story I have in mind relates to one of the wives of the Sanzibar Sultan, falling in love with a Portugese soldier". I requested Hassan to relate to me the story that promised to be arresting and attractive.

Any Arab will only be pleased by a request to narrate a story. They are all borne out of the culture of a Thousand and One Nights full of wondrous stories. So it is no wonder!

Hassan kept silent... may be in preparation for narrating a long story!

It seemed as if the moon light had lessened in intensity. It also appeared that the fort had moved away in the semi darkness. Slightly warm breeze from the sea kept embracing us every now and then. Behind the verandah where we were seated could be heard some movements – that of bats and weasels. It seemed as if burqua clad women were flying over our heads.

"I am going to tell you a love story that had unfolded in this very same fort two hundred and fifty years ago. Hassan was starting his narration. I lit up another cigarette and sat straight, eager to listen to a new story.

"A large group of Arabs from Oman landed in Mombasa in 25 warships, determined to wrest back power from the Portugese. Among them was my ancestor Abdul Khatheeb. I came to know about these developments from the notes and diaries maintained by him"

Thus, it seemed, Hassan was trying to cloak his story with the suggestion of truth. But the story unfolded as if Hassan had been witness to the string of events along with Khatheeb.

"We landed in Mombasa, captured the ancient Fort Joseph and set up camp there. Even before that we had let loose a terrible attack on the city of Mombasa. Following our attack a few black people and their families who had been converted into Christianity by the Portugese as well as some of the paid servants of the Portugese along with a few Europeans had taken refuge in the Fort Jesus. They numbered around two thousand, including women and children. Portugese soldiers in the fort numbered around a hundred.

They had expected Oman Arabs to directly unleash an attack on the Fort Jesus. There idea was to shoot at them when they reached the fort gates. The ammunition available with the Portugese was far more powerful than those with the Arabs.

But we did not attack Fort Jesus. We had decided on another

strategy. We had decided to lay siege on the Fort Jesus!

Thus we were able to isolate the Portugese and the natives who had sided with them right inside the fort itself. We prevented all the ways and means through which they could get food and water. We suspected that the Portugese may try to bring in more soldiers and ammunition from Mombasa in the African mainland. We systematically destroyed all their plans. Instead of the land in Mombasa, all that the Portugese soldiers ever saw was the frightening depths of the ocean. Not a single Portugese were ready to fight with us in the sea; such was our reputation as born sea farers!

We were daily enjoying magnificent dinners in Fort Joseph, while the Portugese and their accomplices in Fort Jesus were daily dying, as if they were cattle, stricken with some infectious disease.

Hassan gave his narration a dramatic pause. He looked around with his sole seeing eye. All that could be heard was the beatings of the wings of bats and weasals who had made the enormous banyan tree in the fort their permanent abode.

“Let the embargo and siege of the Fort Jesus continue. Let us go and see what is happening in the harem of the Sanzibar Sultan!” Hassan made a change to the setting of the story!!

“Zanzibar was a land that had become wealthy by the slave trade. It was the land of scented cloves as well as black beauties. Their, in the harem of the Sultan, his latest wife Karamboo (meaning clove in their language) was reclining in a sandal cot, crying into the soft, downy pillows. In the ceiling, a small love bird was flitting among the thousand and one ornamental glasses attached to the chandelier.

Beside her, on the floor, was seated like an immovable urn, a huge black man!

In the hands of the crying begum could be seen a letter, drenched in tears! It had been delivered from Mombasa by the black man. It was a private message sent by Captain Iago, one of the Portugese soldiers who had been caught in the Fort Jesus.

Begum brushed aside her tears and reread the letter once more. In it was written thus:

"Dear Begum,

My ardent kisses on your hand that is as soft as the softest blue petals of the purest kind!

I have no idea whatsoever whether you will be receiving this letter or not. Even if you get this letter, there is no guarantee at all whether I will be alive then or not! I myself, some fifty Portugese soldiers as well as more than a thousand natives have been caught in the Fort Jesus in Mombasa as the result of the siege laid by the Oman Arab soldiers. Our position is much worse than prisoners of the worst kind. Prisoners will get food and water at regular intervals. For us even water is not available!

The soldiers from Oman, who are comfortably ensconced in the Fort Joseph are making us waste our arms and ammunitions using one ploy or another. We have no way of replenishing them from anywhere what so ever. All routes of aid or contact with the Fort Jesus has been embargoed by the Oman Arabs. We have heard that they have also attacked and sunk a fleet of ships that had come from Mozambique to help us.

Sans arms, ammunition or food, we have all become walking ghosts. Communicable diseases are fast depleting our numbers. The plan of the Arabs is to starve us into death. We are not even able to imagine how long we will be able to undergo the strain of this deadly embargo. Nineteen Portugese soldiers have already died. By the time this letter reaches you more of us might have lost their lives. Among them could be your old friend Iago! (If it happens thus, then consider this letter as my farewell message!)

There is only one person who can help us out at this juncture – the Sanzibar Sultan! It is with this faint hope that I am writing this letter. You are now the new dearest wife of the Sultan, aren't you? If you can use your influence the Sultan will be ready to send some Arab soldiers to help us out of the embargo. Will you do so? If it is not possible, just forget it. Forget Iago too.

Yours,

Iago Viaz

(Captain)

Kissing the letter, Karamboo burst into a fresh volley of tears. She could see the face of Iago awaiting sure death in Fort Jesus, in her mind's eye; she could also hear the feeble request for help reflected in those blue eyes!

Karamboo remembered having first seen the handsome Portugese soldier in a native dance hall almost five years back. She had been one of the more famous dancers in Sanzibar at that time. When her dance was over, a tall, lean handsome Portugese youth and walked on to the stage from the audience, kissed her hands and requested her to dance with him. More than his physical handsomeness, what attracted Karamboo was the humility and the loving behavior of the youth.

Europeans usually never used to frequent native dance halls. They had a kind of aversion, coupled with derision, towards the uncivilized dance forms of the natives. Even if they put in an appearance at native dance halls, it will be in a totally inebriated state, with the sole intention of physically raping the dancer. This young man was not drunk; in his blue eyes could be seen reflected a love of humanity and high cultural sensitivity. Iago and Karamboo danced hand in hand. The other audience beat their hands to rhythm. Iago had fallen in love with Karamboo!

Karamboo caressed the ring on her finger and kissed it gently. It was a present from Iago. She remembered Iago telling her the story of the precious stone embedded in the ring. The stone had earlier been part of the necklace that had adorned the idol of one of the more famous temples in India. The Portugese had ransacked the temple, took possession of all the gold and ornaments that had been amassed there, destroyed the idol and finally placed a wooden cross in the temple premises, before returning to their home land. Iago had also recounted how all the Europeans in the group which had ransacked the temple, all save Iago himself had been killed in an attack by Oman sailors in the deep ocean. She also remembered Iago declaring that he will go back to India, and then come back to Sanzibar with sacks full of precious jewels and ornaments and will place them at the feet of Karamboo.

A thought passed through her mind – Iago, the only European to have survived after ransacking the costly ornaments from an Indian idol, is alas now starving to death at the Jesus Fort in Mombasa.

She glowered at the ring on her finger. Is it an accursed one? she was all in doubt. No, she reassured herself. The Sanzibar Sultan had met her just the day after she had received this ring from Iago. The Sultan had unhesitatingly declared her his wife the very next day and had taken her into his harem. But even before that Iago had left for India.

There had not been a single night ever since, when Karamboo's thoughts had not hovered around Iago. She continued to be hankering after Iago's embraces, even in the midst of all the luxuries in the sultan's palace.

She sat up in the bed and considered her options. This was not the time to indulge in sweet memories about love. It was dangerous even to have such thoughts. Some course of action has to be thought about. The black servant was waiting for an answer.

She thought of many possible solutions. The possibility of the Sanzibar Sultan sending his army to fight against Oman Arabs in favour of Portugese soldiers couldn't even be thought of. It would also be dangerous to consider requesting the sultan for his help in rescuing Iago from the Jesus Fort without fighting the Oman Arabs. The sultan was already in the know of the fact that Karamboo had a lover named Iago and that he was a Portugese soldier. If the sultan ever comes to know of the contents of this letter, Karamboo's head too would roll, doubtless!

This line of thinking made her head spin. More than her love and regards for a former lover, what made Karamboo more excited and ready for action was the fact that the European lover had approached her in search of solution to a life and death problem. The fact that here were natives too, on the verge of the death, in the same fort did not even cross her mind. All that she could see in her mind's eye was Iago's face! How can she keep quiet when the very same lips that had covered her face, eyes and breasts with a virtually unstoppable shower of kisses was in imminent danger of being dried up due to lack of water? The blue eyes that had been full of affection for her was now staring at death, and can she keep still? The lone light of hope and delivery in those eyes was Karamboo...

She was brought back to the present with a shudder when she heard someone knocking on her door. She understood that it could be none other than the sultan. Gesturing that he should .keep completely quiet, Karamboo rolled up the black servant into a tight coil made out of one of the costly rugs in the room. After adroitly hiding the letter from Iago in one of the numerous silk pillows that adorned the palatial bed room, Karamboo went and opened the door for the Sultan with an expectant smile and with dancing steps.

The sultan couldn't suppress his laughter on seeing her dance. "Has the dearest wife of the Sanzibar Sultan been affected by the ghost of dancing? What is happening?"- He placed his arms on her shoulders and asked with smiling eyes.

Lightly caressing the sultan's hairy chest with gossamer like finger strokes, Karamboo led him to the huge bed that adorned the room.

"I was asleep a short while back and in my sleep I did see an astonishing dream", said Karamboo in reply to the Sultan's query. "The setting was a divine garden. There were only the two of us there. On a sandal wood table in the middle of the lawns that dotted the garden could be seen golden cups of the highest quality Shiras wines. Sipping the wine glass your highness asked me "Karamboo, how long can you dance sans any break?" "I can dance until you ask me to stop. You can try!"I replied.

"You were determined to test me and asked me to start dancing. I started dancing and you enjoyed my performance, all the while slowly sipping the wine. My dance and your drinking continued and at one point you fell asleep. I continued with my dancing, waiting for your order to stop....You knocked on the door at this juncture and waking up from my sleep I welcomed you, still dancing!"

The Sultan shook with laughter. He said "it is an astonishing dream indeed! I have come to make your dream real! I intend to sit here and enjoy your dancing, while tasting the best of Shiraz wines!"

Karamboo embraced him with all her might, and clinging on to his neck she said "I will dance till you order me to stop!"

The sultan started drinking from a pot and Karamboo began dancing on the floor of the room!

Hassan stopped his narration. He looked around again, as if expecting someone. At that point the bell began to toll from the Jesus Fort, yet again. One, two.... Hassan shut his ears in pain! His face shriveled with fright and pain. The clock struck ten.

It seemed that Hassan had forgotten all about going to the cinema at 9 30 pm. Indeed, I did pray that he forget it. I did not want to allow him to leave me in the midst of this exciting story.

The silence lasted only a minute, but it seemed as if a century had passed by. In the slanting moon rays, the shadow of the Jesus Fort assumed the shape of a reclining elephant! The shadows of trees intermingled one to one and seemed to approach as if they were octopuses waiting to catch us. Bats continued their flights above us, eerily resembling women clad in black burquas. In this scene of quiet darkenesses of various kinds, the only ray of brightness as the glistening of Hassan's single eye! The eye glowed green in the moon light and shadows, as if it was the eye of a tiger!

"Hey Mr Hassan, you have left Karamboo dancing in front of the Sultan...." I tried to remind Hassan about the story.

"Yes, yes", Hassan responded as if he had just awoken from deep thought. He looked at me absentmindedly and then shut his sole eye. His face seemed attractive when the eye was shut! He continued speaking, the eye still closed.

"Let Karamboo continue her dance in front of the Sultan! In the meanwhile, let us find out what has happened in the Jesus Fort."

◆

MASKS ON THE MARCH

"What was the state of affairs in Jesus Fort? The inside of the fort had changed into a truly barbaric world. The simple fact that hunger and thirst affects the White man and the Black equally created myriad problems there. Whose lives should be protected - those of the Europeans or those of the native Africans? Without any doubt, the Whiteman decided that the lives of the Europeans should be protected. The White religious propagators had instilled among the black population the belief that the black men were fated to be ruled over by the white men. But when hunger calls at their door steps, some of the converted black people were not ready to follow these teachings!

Physically, it was the black people who had been able to withstand the pangs of hunger better than the white men. At the same time, guns and ammunitions were totally under the white master's control. Thus it inevitably came to the point that confrontation between the Europeans and natives in the Jesus Fort was unavoidable, taking into consideration the demand for food and water. The Portugese were waiting for the first move from the natives. They thought that the numbers of the black, native community could be considerably lessened in that scenario. They also thought that the chances of the remaining people being able to remain alive can also be increased by this strategy.

With this is mind, the Portugese tried their maximum to provoke the natives into action. When an internal revolution was slowly brewing inside the fort, another danger, in the guise of plague, also raised its ugly head inside the fort. Like hunger, plague also did not consider Europeans and natives separately. The terrible communicative disease caused death among the Europeans and the natives in equal measure. Many people on both sides fell dead with out assistance from any war or revolt.

At the same time, Sheikh Shamsudeen and his soldiers were sitting for dinner inside the other fort – the Joseph fort. They were exchanging funny stories and jokes about the terror shown by the Portugese during the Omanese attacks!

Noori Yoosuf was the comedian in the group of soldiers headed by Shamsuden. He enacted for the whole group the final moments of a Portugese soldier who had taken a bullet in his buttocks. On hearing this, the pot bellied Sheikh couldn't withhold his laughter. Morsels of food and pan could be seen coming out of the Sheikh's mouth and falling on the dresses and faces of the audience when he was in laughing fits! Every one acted as if they were under an epileptic attack.

Days went by! One day, the excitement in the Joseph Fort, where Oman soldiers were camping appeared to be more than normal. An almost festive mood could be discerned in the fort. One more Portugese boat had been attacked by the Oman soldiers. When they were preparing to celebrate the victory, yet another Oman ship arrived carrying more food and drinks. They decided to kill a camel and celebrate the twin developments.

It was a moon lit night. A group of burqua clad women, led by an Arab youth passed by in front of the Joseph court. Hameed, the old guard at the fort gates watched them with interest. There was nothing suspicious in that. It was common to see burqua clad women, especially Muslim women, going to visit relatives and friends or simply wandering in groups, on moon lit nights.

Hameed, who was watching the movements of the group, suddenly felt suspicious. He detected something irregular as far as the movements of the group were concerned. He found out that they were moving in military style step by step, which was unusual as far as women were concerned. He fired a volley of shots into the air. The burqua clad women weren't affected by the noise. There movements did not change in the least.

Hameed rushed into the fort as if his dress had caught fire. Finding out Shamsudeen he called "rush out! We have been tricked. I have been able to recognize, by the grace of Allah, that a set of burqua clad women who had passed in front of our fort are actually soldiers in disguise. They are walking with military precision and they are being led by an Arab youth!"

Shamsudeen and others immediately rushed out. By then the burqua clad group was almost hundred feet the fort gate. Shamsudeen stared at them. He realized that they were walking towards the Jesus fort. They must be Portugese people in disguise trying to help those in the Jesus fort.

He burst out in laughter. "Dear friends, prepare for some amusement after dinner.... Security guard, order the draw bridge at the Jesus fort entrance to be with drawn!"

Three shots were heard from the Joseph Fort. A red light could be seen shining in a particular pattern from the fort – a signal that the draw bridge should be with drawn!

No one should even dream of reaching the Jesus Fort without the knowledge and permission of the authorities in the Joseph Fort! On the road to Jesus Fort, the Arabs had built a moat and a wooden draw bridge across it. The moat had its origin in the sea and it was always full of sea water. No sooner does the guard, at the Jesus Fort gets the necessary command from the Joseph fort, he will wait for the suspicious persons to enter the draw bridge and then he will simply withdraw the latch beneath the bridge. The inevitable result will be a watery grave to all those on the bridge!

In addition, an extensive grid of minute nets was also placed beneath the drawbridge. People were caught in the net, pulled to the shore and tortured also, if the Oman soldiers so desired! It was one of their favorite pastimes!

As was to be expected, the moment the Arab youth and his twelve burqua clad followers entered the draw bridge, it was opened and all of them fell head long into the sea water. Those who hesitated at the entrance to the bridge were physically pushed into the moat by the Oman soldiers who had followed them from the Joseph Fort.

Chanting some rural ditties, the Omanese pulled the net to the shore. The burqua people were shivering from cold and fright. Some had developed breathing problems because of having drunk sea water to excess. They were feeling nauseated because of extended stomachs and they some how wanted to come out of the burquas.

With the burquas removed, the Oman Arabs were in for a big surprise. All they could see was a set of Arab soldiers from some other country, staring at them with shame and sheepishness! They could only stand and stare foolishly at their leader. The leader was sans head gear, but her hair covered two mounds of flesh that adorned her breasts! The burqua clad women had turned out to be men, while the lone Arab youth had been transformed into a woman!! Wonder of wonders!!

Some of the Arab soldiers from Oman were not able to withstand the surprise. They shouted "it is the work of the devil! Beware!"

The usual practice was to make the enemies caught in the net walk nude through the city. But the Oman soldiers were not able to decide what is to be done with this particular group. This was the first time that a woman had fallen into the net!

Finally they presented all of them in front of Shamsudeen. He looked over the black soldiers and the black and blue beauty with interest. They were twenty one in number. Shamsudeen felt flabbergasted. He couldn't understand what was happening. All he could understand, with certainty was that they were all Arabs. But why were they helping the Portugese? It remained a mystery.

Out of frustration Shamsudeen shouted "who are you? Where are you coming from?" No one answered. He fixed his sights on the woman. She was shivering from head to toe.

Shamsudeen rubbed his forehead in weariness and ordered his soldiers to provide the captive Arabs with fresh clothes and then bring them back before him.

One of the eunuchs in the fort took charge of them. Within half an hour they returned, all clad in white, free flowing kurthees. Since female dresses were practically unavailable in the fort, the woman was also dressed in the same manner. Only her overflowing hair that masked her breasts revealed her real identity.

"Who are you people? Where are you coming from," Shamsudeen repeated his questions. No reply yet again

A small crowd, consisting of ordinary soldiers, servants of the court as well as Abdul Khatheeb, had gathered around to see what was happening. Suddenly one of the servants moved forward, bowed to Shamsudeen and said "may the Sheikh live long, with the blessings of Allah! Will you permit this humble slave to say a few words?" "Yes…." agreed the Sheikh.

"I recognize this Arab lady. She is the latest begum of the Sanzibar Sultan. Her name is Karamboo. Before being married to the Sultan, she had been the most famous dancer in Sanzibar."

Shamsudeen sat as if in shock, his mouth wide open in wonder! "Oh! The Begum of the Sanzibar Sultan! Is this true?" He asked the lady, in calm and measured voice, belying hos excitement.

"Yes", replied she. "I am Karamboo, the begum of the Sanzibar Sultan." The huge hall reverberated with her clear, bell like voice. "And who are these?" he asked again pointing at the others. He gave the reply also "Oh yes, who else but the soldiers of the Sultan!" She had no hesitancy in confirming it.

"Why did you come to Mombasa? Were you thinking of helping those Portuguese swines?"

"Now, now! Your last words are not completely true." Karamboo raised her voice slightly in disagreement.

"Then pray tell me the real reason for your coming down here?" Shamsudeen repeated his question.

"I had come down to visit an old friend of mine who is suffering in Fort Jesus", Karamboo replied.

"And who is this friend?", Shamsudeen persisted in his questioning.

Karamboo sat mum, fixing here eyes on the ground. The sheikh repeated his question, a trifle irritated.. "Who is it?"

Karamboo's voice trembled when she said "Captain Iago!"

◆

THE JEWELS OF THE CEMETERY

The shadow of the Jesus Fort that was falling on the lawns loomed ominous to my eyes. The sea breeze slightly strengthened. Hassan suddenly got up from his seat and just as suddenly resumed the sitting position.

He focused his one eye on my face and asked rather roughly "where did we stop?"

"Karamboo is being questioned in Fort Joseph. She says that she had come to the jesus Fort to see a friend named Captain Iago" I replied.

Hassan responded "Ok, OK! Let the questioning continue. Let us go and see what is happening to Iago".

Iagao and seventeen others were the only Portugese people remaining alive in the fort. They themselves were not leading a harmonious life. Rather, it seemed that only hunger, disease and death were the only entities that were living in harmony in the fort.

The Portugese soldiers in the fort had acquired a large number of precious stones during their raids in numerous temples of India. The most valuable collection was in the possession of Iago. His friends too knew this. All those jewels were not owned by Iago. Man's greed regarding wealth and jewels has a history as long as the existence of the world. Countless are the wars and murders that have taken place for these objects. They still continue.

Man has been destroyed in his attempts to own wealth and jewels. But the gold and jewels lying hidden in the earth has no limit. These bits of metal often indulge in a game of hide and seek just to provoke man into quarreling with each other and killing one another. Gold, jewels, diamonds all are constantly on the move – from one man to another; from one safe vault to another; nay, even from one country to another! And in the course of such movements and relocations, they result in the death of many.

Portugese soldiers attacked and ransacked countless ornaments that adorned the various temples in India. They were not able to transport them safely to their mother land and instead they got stuck in a fort in Mombasa.

One soldier named Perera had in his possession a diamond that was in the shaped like an egg. It had earlier adorned as the third eye of the Shiva idol in a temple in Malabar. Another by name Lawrence used to carry a small box in his pockets. It was said that the small intricately crafted box was full of diamonds of all shapes and sizes! Pinto, another soldier owned an over coat, the buttons of which were all emeralds! Thus it was that the Portugese soldiers of the Jesus fort, one and all, were in possession of immense wealth which they hid in whatever way possible. It was also rumored that some had even buried their possessions in various pits dug in various parts of the fort!

With the embargo of the Jesus Fort at its peak, all that the

Portugese soldiers could think of was about ensuring the safety and security of their jewel hordes! They were intensely suspicious of each other. When epidemics ruled the fort, when death was performing its hideous dance in front of them, the faces of these Portugese soldiers turned into embodiments of greed and selfishness. They were even ready to go to the extent of killing their friend or brother and taking away the jewels owned by them too!

The Oman soldiers had also heard rumors about the huge haul of priceless metals in the possession of the Portugese soldiers. They dreamt about the golden moment when all the Portugese soldiers in the Jesus Fort would fall dead, leaving them the gold haul! In their dreams, the Jesus Fort appeared a fort of diamonds!

Parera, who owned the egg shaped diamond, was at this death bed. He had safely preserved the diamond, with the only intention of presenting it to his girl friend in Lisbon. All that Perera could think of when he had ransacked the temple and destroyed the Shiva idol in Malabar, were the raising breasts of his sweet heart. A recurring dream of his had been the pendent bearing the diamond hanging low in the middle of his girl friend's breasts! When he became sure that death was approaching, he called Captain Iago to his side. He raised the diamond and told him:

"Captain Iago, listen to me carefully. I wish to entrust the ownership of this diamond to someone else at the time of my death. I desire that you become the new owner of this precious stone. There is a reason for this – you are the person I hate the most among all the Portugese inside the Jesus Fort. Yes - I hate you the most, Captain

Iago!"

Saying this, Perera gave vent to a murderous laugh! "This is an accursed jewel. Let it be with you!" Extending the hand holding the diamond, Perea breathed his last. Iago was astounded. He felt ashamed of taking ownership of the diamond after hearing Perera's words. But this is an invaluable jewel and how can anyone refuse it? Is it indeed accursed? Nonsense! Perera had gone mad. Each and every one who died in the fort becomes mad in the end. A madness engendered by jewels!

Iago walked towards his room, the diamond held in his hands. Actually he was not walking; he was crawling, with fatigue! It was days since he had anything substantial to eat. He had become just an emaciated collection of bones! He was even ready to trade the diamond stone in lieu of just a piece of bread.

In the fort he had seen many instances of people turning into demons as a result of hunger. Perera, who had bequeathed him the diamond, had been one such demon. Perera was even reputed to have killed a small child inside his room, when he couldn't contain his hunger! It was rumored that it took two weeks for Perera to eat up the child completely.

Iago entered his room. He closed the door securely and removed a blanket that had been thrown in a heap in one corner of the room. Then he took out an old cloth bundle that he had hidden there and poured its contents on to the blanket.

The room, which had seemed dark and remote, suddenly became as well lit as a room full of powerful lamps. The bundle was full of many kinds of gems, jewels and stones. Iago stared at them. His eyes grew dim because of the power of the rays emanated by these stones. His head began to turn.

He became confused. His mind was assailed by confusing and even opposing streams of thought. He alternately assumed consciousness and fell unconscious. One moment he felt that the stones were keys to a bright future; the next moment he saw them as the barren teeth of some long dead soul! He felt that jewels had turned into pools of blood, while diamonds had transformed into lakes of tears! All in all he felt himself to have been caught up in a den of death! He wanted to cry out; but demonic laughter alone was he able to produce. Muttering something repeatedly, Iago threw his latest addition into the blanket and tied up the bundle securely!

Madness was slowly spreading all over his brains. His physical strength also increased with the spread of madness. Carrying the bundle of jewels on his head, Iago wandered here and there around the fort.

Suddenly he stopped; he thought he heard someone crying from somewhere far away. Then he realized that the crying was emanating from one corner of the fort where some tribal nomads had set up a temporary camp. It was a tribal woman giving birth to a dead child. The woman also died after the delivery. Iago stared at the still child. It was a white child; in the moon light the blood covered child seemed as if it were someone's heart just wrenched out and thrown away.

Iago felt dizzy. He went and sat under a tree. He felt himself going down into the earth. He realized that he had been sitting on a pile of earth that had just been dug up. It was a fresh pit, dug up by someone quite recently. Using his hands Iago removed some of the soil and he was able to locate a jar in the pit. He emptied it and a handful of jewels splattered on to the soil, blinding him by their brilliance. Iago stared at them, laughed uproariously and transferred them to his blanket. Now he transferred the blanket to a position under his arm and continued his wanderings here and there in the compound.

By and by he reached the small cemetery in the fort. It was a temporary one, used to bury those who had recently passed away inside the fort. Fernandez and Sebastian, Iago's close friends were among those who had been buried there. Fernandez had died because of the plague.

Iago knew that the collection of jewels owned by Fernandez had been buried somewhere inside the fort. He also knew that Fernadez had taken enough precautions so that it would be extremely difficult for anyone to uncover the horde. Iago suddenly realized that he was standing on the top of world's wealthiest horde of jewels and precious stone, because many a Portugese soldier had hidden their hoarded wealth inside the environs of the Jesus Fort. He did not feel like moving away from the fort. Still clutching the blanket consisting of the jewels safely under his arm, Iago unknowingly fell into a slumber.

◆

THE SHIPS ARE COMING

And then said Hassan: "Now let us go to the Joseph Fort. There Sheikh Shamsudeen is still interrogating Begum Karamboo".

When Karamboo's lips uttered the name of Iago, Shamsudeen reacted automatically "that Portugese swine!" Then he asked Karamboo in the roughest tone possible "So you are siding with the Portugese, who are born enemies of the Islam, is it so?"

Karamboo's voice wavered when she replied " I do not have any intention of quarreling with my Islam brethren. My only aim is to help a friend of mine!"

The Sheikh couldn't help raising his voice; "We are intelligent enough to reason out that this could not be your sole reason. What is the necessity of bringing 20 soldiers, disguised as ladies into the fort? Your intention could only have been to help the remaining Portugese soldiers escape, securely covered up in these very same burquas? The Sanzibar soldiers were to be left in the fort to attack us ... excellent idea!"

Karamboo did not give any reply. The Sheikh growled with anger and frustration. "Let me ask you one thing. Does the Sanzibar Sultan know that you have embarked upon this dangerous trip?"

Karamboo replied in tear tinged words "No; the expedition was mounted under my sole responsibility. Now I have forsaken both the Sanzibar Sultan and his kingdom by doing this."

Sheikh glanced at Abdul Khatheeb and remarked "did you hear the words of the Begum of Sanzibar?" "Of course", replied Khatheeb. "A woman who has fallen in love and a drunken camel are the same. No one in the whole world will be able to control them!"

The Sheikh turned his attention back to Karamboo. "You are saying that you have forsaken the Sanzibar Sultan and the country for the sake of your lover Iago. What guarantee do you have that Iago is still alive?" Karamboo lowered her face and murmured "that is what I firmly believe!"

Next the Sheikh turned his attention to the other soldiers from Sanzibzr. "Do you have anything to say?" The head of the group of soldiers said "We are innocent. We have started according to the orders of the Sanzibar Sultan - that is what Begum has made us believe!" The soldiers from Oman called out "Oh! She is a traitor!"

The Sheikh again turned his attention to Karamboo. "Do you have any evidence that Iago is still alive inside the Jesus Fort?" "Yes. I did receive a letter written by him", replied Karamboo. "Much might have happened after that. Many people have died inside the fort as a result of the plague. How can you be sure that Iago has not been a victim of the plague? Have you thought about what your fate would be if you are unable to locate Iago or if he has already died?" "I have not thought on those lines. I still believe he is alive!" She remained firm. "May your faith protect you", replied the Sheikh. "But we can see you only as a person who has acted as a spy for the Portugese against us!"

The Sheikh then held some private consultations with Khatheeb. Returning, he told Karamboo "Karamboo, Oh Begum of the Sanzibar Sultan, listen to my words carefully! You are to be beheaded; that is the law of war. There is no way at all for exempting you from this law." Then he turned towards the Sanzibar soldiers, "All of you are innocent. I grant pardon to all! All of you will be recruited into our army!"

Then, a smile hovering on his lips, the Sheikh turned his eyes on to Karamboo. "Oh! Begum! I, Sheikh Shamsudeen of Oman Army can only admire your bravery. I also praise your intelligence and ability. I admire your loyalty to the one whom you love. Taking into consideration all these factors I am hereby ordering that you shall be allowed to spend one night with Iago, before you are beheaded!"

Karamboo stood stunned when she heard the orders of the Sheikh. Then she asked; "I do not understand the meaning of your order. Will you allow me into Jesus Fort? How will I find out Iago?"

The Sheikh responded. "It can be done exactly the way you had planned. You send an envoy with your message to Iago. Ask him to come and meet you in a lonely spot on the Kalindini sea shore."

Karamboo remained silent for a while. Then she asked in a low voice, "Will you betray me? Will you order Iago to be killed?" "No. You needn't have any suspicions" replied the Sheikh. We Arabs have a culture of never killing our guests or those who have come asking for shelter. "Not only that", he glanced at Khatheeb, "if it is proved that Iago is as much in love with you as you are with him, I can promise that I will let him leave!"

Karamboo thought for a while. She tried to analyze the Sheikh's order in various ways. She was not able to understand his real objective. Finally she decided to go ahead, come what may. Each day alive is precious, she thought. And if I am able to see Iago once again before death, then that could be my biggest fortune!

The Sheikh also encouraged her. He ordered her to write a message and dictated the words. An ink pot, sharpened feather and paper appeared as if from nowhere! "I have received your letter. I have reached the Kalindini coast along with twenty disguised Sanzibar soldiers. You start with the person who is bringing you this message, disguised using the burqua he will provide. It will be dangerous for us to come inside the fort. There is a chance that the Oman soldiers may find us out. Once you have escaped safely, we can try and bring out all the remaining European soldiers outside to safety. We can start for Mosambique tonight itself. I am waiting for you in one of the lonely caves of Kalindini,

Your own, Karamboo".

After the message had been composed the Shekh asked Karamboo whether she had any memento to be passed on along with the letter. She immediately took off the bejeweled ring presented by Iago himself and handed it over to the Sheikh. He, on his part, immediately dispatched a loyal servant to the Jesus Fort with the assignment of finding out Iago and handing over the letter and memento to him.

No sooner had the messenger left, the Sheikh took all the twenty Sanzibar soldiers and Karamboo to the coast of Kalindini. The ship in which Karamboo had arrived was lying there. He ordered his own soldiers to immediately board the ship and told them to see that the ship was kept in readiness to cast off to the sea immediately. Then he, accompanied by Khatheeb and Karamboo, entered one of the lonely cottages on the coast. Then he advised her as follows:

"I, accompanied by Khatheeb will be waiting in the next room. You are not to give any signs, during your conversations with Iago, that there is anybody else in this house except you two. Remember that each of your words and gestures are being watched by me and Khatheeb in the very next room. If you attempt anything foolish or fool hardy, your life will be forfeited; so will your lover's!"

Karamboo bowed her head in agreement.

The Sheikh and Khatheeb stood waiting in one of the smaller rooms of the cottage to catch a glimpse of Iago. The cottage was one where cattle were kept during peace time. It was past midnight. The Kalaindini sea appeared like a wide court yard filled with mud. Every now and then, the low pitched hum of the waves could be heard reverberating. It seemed as if an ogre was letting out a deep breath. The shadows of the palm trees that dotted the coast seemed as if they were the long hairs of a witch spread out to dry!

It was quite some time after that they espied two forms approaching the cottage, taking care to be well hidden by the palms. the one behind was dressed in a burqua. Both of them were moving very carefully.

The Shekh whispered into Khatheeb's ears "our strategy seems to have worked out!" Yes, both the shapes entered the cottage. They walked towards the room in which Karamboo was waiting. After letting the burqua clad shape into the room, the other person returned.

The person removed the burqua and out was revealed just a bag of bones. "Iago, Iago! My love, my love!" cried Karamboo, embracing the skeleton like person. The Sheikh and Khatheeb were not in the least worried about what Karamboo was saying. They were concerned about the bundle in Iago's hands.

They noticed that even in the midst of all the embracing and endearments by Karamboo, Iago was holding on to the bundle with firm hands. Both the Sheikh as well as Khatheeb felt elated. "All the invaluable gold ornaments in India are glowing like fire inside the bundle! Those jewels have come here in search of us", whispered Khatheeb. The Sheikh remarked "but for this strategy we would never have got all the treasure in one place, isn't it?"

Suddenly a hue and cry could be heard from the coast. Both the Sheikh as well as Khatheeb was startled. They felt that some altercation was increasing in intensity. The opened the spy hole in one of the walls and could espy a fleet of vessels in the sea and a multitude of soldiers rushing on to the land. "Were they Portugese from Mozambique?" the Sheikh wondered. "No", he soon realized. The soldiers were Arabs, Arabs from Sanzibar. The ships belonged to the Sanzibar Sultan!

◆

JEWELS LOST IN THE SEA

The Sheikh couldn't believe that the ships which had come ashore where those belonging to the Sanzibar Sultan. He was able to discern from afar that some sort of skirmish was going on in the sea shore. He stood, looking towards the sea shore, slightly apprehensive and slightly anxious. He could see fire burning; he could hear cries of victory; he could understand the soft sobs of the vanquished! He understood that a war was afoot – but who was fighting whom? Are Portugese ships involved in the battle? He had no idea at all!

The shout of exhilaration produced by the skeleton in the next room however alarmed the Sheikh. He wondered what could be the meaning of the shouting. The Sheikh felt unable to move far away from the skeleton like shape of Iago who was still clutching the bundle full of jewels under his arms. The Sheikh's thoughts had been filled for several months with the thoughts of the huge cache of gold and jewels hidden in various parts of the Jesus Fort. It hadn't been totally impossible to attack the Fort and kill all the Portugese soldiers there. But then no clue to the whereabouts of the treasures in the fort would have remained. That was the only reason why the Sheikh desisted from taking that course of action.

Right now the treasures are out in the open. They are now in a position where if he stretched his arms he will be able to touch them! If his attention wavered even for the fraction of a second, they would vanish forever. All these thoughts flashed through the Sheikh's mind within the fraction of a second! He decided to send Khatheeb to the Kalindini coast to find out what was happening.

In the next room, the skeleton and Karamboo were standing face to face. It seemed as if all the commotions in the sea coast hadn't affected them in the least! But the Sheikh had eyes only for the bundle. He knew that the contents of the bundle would be more than enough to buy not one , but many an empire. He had often dreamt of the countless invaluable stones and jewels that had adorned the eyes, necks and breasts of Hindu Gods and Goddesses. The Sheikh sighed at the realization that he had never been able to go anywhere in Hindusthan. But the consolation was that these very same treasures had come to him here in the court yard of Fort Jesus! He was impatient to see the contents of the bundle and he glanced at the lovers a little harshly. They did not seem to have any plans of separating from each other!

The Sheeikh thought to himself: Poor Karamboo! She might be thinking that the Portugese soldier will be ready to perform a bigger sacrifice than the one she had done for him. We can only wait and see!

Shamsudeen congratulated himself for having so effectively set uop a love test for Iago and Karamboo! As soon as a sign was given, a platoon of soldiers were waiting to whisk Karamboo away, within the flutter of an eye. (They might be waiting some where within hearing!) When caught by Arab soldiers, Karamboo will natuarally cry out for help. Then we can see how Iago will react to an attack, a kidnapping attaempt, that takes place right in front of him.

In addition, the Sheikh had already ordered the leader of the twenty soldiers in the ship to call out that it will be immediately leaving for Mozambique. What will be Iago's decision? Will he stick to the stand that he won't embark on the ship sans his lover or will he take his chance and try to escape with his hoard of jewels?

But poor Iago! He has no idea that the ship was going to turn towards Fort Joseph. It will be at this juncture that Karamboo realizes the real nature of Iago's love for her. The Sheikh couldn't help smiling to himself when he imagined the scene in which Karamboo meets Iago again inside the Fort Joseph later!

When he realized for the first time that the skeleton was Iago himself, the Sheikh had felt extremely disturbed. He really thought that Karamboo might forget all about her love with Iago and flee from the scene. But what has happened was just the opposite. She had tightly embraced the very same skeleton and clearly demonstrated the strength of her love.

The Sheikh was disturbed again because of the repeated roars from the next room. He couldn't in the least fathom what they signified. Suddenly he heard the gasps of Khatheeb as he came running up from the coast. He wanted to say something, but his voice seemed struck somewhere in the throat! Shaking his shoulders violently, the Sheikh asked Khatheeb again and again "What's happening on the coast?"

At last Khtheeb gasped out an answer "War.... it's war! A war is being fought right now between the Arabs from Sanzibar and those from Oman. They have killed everyone abroad the ship in which Karamboo had come. The remaining ten ships and the soldiers they carried are ready to move towards the Joseph Fort, under the command of the Sultan himself!"

The Sheikh couldn't believe his ears. There was no earthly reason whatsoever for a war to break out between the Sanzibar and Oman soldiers.

In the midst of all this confusion, forgetting all about Karamboo and Iago, the Sheikh wailed at the top of his voice "Khatheeb, is this true? Or are you mad?" "Oh, respected sir, I saw this with my own eyes. Right now the fight is going on between the second troop of Oman soldiers whom you had send from the Joseph Fort and the soldiers from Sanzibar. Once the fight is over they are sure to move towards the Joseph Fort. Go, go quickly there!"

The Sheikh was aghast. Placing a palm across his chest he said, "Khatheeb, Joseph Fort is a place sans any leader now. Pray, do you have any idea why the Sanzibar Sultan has turned against us?"

Wiping the streaming sweat from his forehead, Khatheeb said "Oh! I forgot to tell you in the midst of all this excitement. The reason for this attack is none other than this very same Karamboo!" "Karamboo?" repeated the Sheikh.

"Yes. None other than her! The Sanzibar Sultan has been made to believe that Oman Arabs had attacked the ship and had carried away Karamboo! He believes that Karamboo is in Joseph Fort and hence he will be here soon!"

Beating on his forehead the Sheikh murmured "Everything has gone wrong! He felt infuriated when Khatheeb said that when Arab fights Arab the Portugese will escape from the fort. He asked in frustration "don't you have anything to say about Arabs dying needlessly on both sides? This has to be stopped, no doubt."

"Then come!" said Khatheeb. "All the time we are sitting here and talking, many more Oman Arabs might be falling down fighting. If we can present Karamboo to the Sanzibar Sultan, all these troubles will be over!"

"But will she agree to this? She had forsaken both the Sultan and Sanzibar for the sake of Iago, didn't she?"

"That may be correct. But it is doubtless that the Sultan is still all eyes for her. He believes that the Oman Arabs have kidnapped her."

"Oh, I don't think that she will leave this skeleton", the Sheikh shook his head in desperation. Khatheeb was all for immediately killing the Portugese swine and taking away Karamboo.

But the Sheikh couldn't agree to this suggestion. "I had promised that I won't kill the Portugese soldier whom I myself had invited to Joseph Fort" "Then why not take away Karamboo and hand her over to the Sultan", Khatheeb offered another suggestion. "What is to be done with the skeleton then?" asked the Sheikh. Khatheeb had a readymade solution. "You have to forcefully wrench the blanket bundle from him and send him back to Jesus Fort, that's all!"

No sooner had Khatheeb raised this suggestion, a group of Sanzibar soldiers, armed to the very teeth, had encircled the house. The Sheikh and Khatheeb cowered in one corner and waited with bated breaths. The soldiers entered the middle room where Iago was conversing with Karamboo. They were led by none other than the Sanzibar Sultan. But all they could see in the room was the sleeping form of Karamboo. The skeleton had magically disappeared, as if into thin air!

The last watch of the night was approaching. The Sanzibar Sultan and his soldiers were returning in high spirits after having vanquished the Omanese and regained Karamboo. The ocean glittered like some strange jewel in the moonlit night. The ships, their sails extended to the fullest extent, resembled lotuses just about to open when the first rays of the sun fell on them. The fleet of ten ships moved steadily in a southern direction.

Karamboo was still lying unconscious in the lap of the Sultan – as if she was tired after continuously dancing, without any break. The Sanzibar soldiers were exchanging stories about the Oman soldiers. Some of them were singing in groups. The notes of these songs spread out and slowly dissolved in the depths of the ocean. In ocean could also be seen huge sharks frolicking amidst the waves.

A skeleton, covered in burqua, and carrying a bundle, was steadily swimming in the wake of the ships! The skeleton was alternately crying and laughing out aloud. But both went unnoticed by the songs of the Sanzibar soldiers.

However, two shapes stood on the shore watching the sight – the Sheikh and Khtaheeb!

◆

THE STORY TELLER'S STORY

Leaving those two shapes, staring at the shining surface of the deep ocean on the sea shore, Hassan brought the story to a conclusion.

I sat staring at the Jesus Fort. In the moon light, it resembled a skeleton, covered up in a burqua!

Hassan shook me firmly and said in a low, but firm voice:

"The spirit of Iago, a skeleton carrying a bundle under its arms, can often can be seen to be loitering in this very fort on some nights. You are sitting here all alone, enjoying the soft sea breeze. Suddenly you see a shape, covered in a burqua coming towards you. You feel being surrounded by the smell of sweet cloves. You will be filled with the sweet expectations that some Mombaza girl is approaching you, in search of company. It slowly comes near you and stands quietly. Then it slowly removes the burqua and you will find yourself staring at a skeleton! It will shake its bundle, holding it near your face and will disappear as suddenly as it had appeared before you!"

When Hassan said this, I had the eerie feeling as if someone had touched my nerves with a cold, but blunt knife! I felt Hassan focusing his only eye on my face, like a powerful searchlight, in an attempt to gauge my reactions! It was then that I noticed a shadow approaching us from a nearby group of trees. It was a burqua clad form!

Hassan was standing, as if oblivious of surroundings, with his gaze focused on me alone. The form came and stood before us. I wanted to raise my arm, but couldn't. I wanted to shout; but no voice seemed to come out of my throat.

Suddenly I could see some lights and sounds emanating from the South east corner of the fort. Sounds of some one wreathing in pain and yet others bellowing in anger could be heard. This was followed by persistent whistling. The burqua clad figure which had stood before seemed to have dissolved into the thin air. Hassan, the story teller also seemed to have disappeared magically!

I wanted to run away from the fort. But I could not even get up and stand. My legs seemed to have become numb. All my nerves seemed to have been tightly bundled up. Some colorful dramas were being enacted in my brain – black burquas, shining jewels, skeletons, ships from Sanzibar, Begum Karamboo – all were dancing together inside my brains! It seemed as if my brains couldn't undergo these feelings anymore. My brain seemed to be shutting down.

I heard sirens being blown. I saw search light beams traversing the coast. I heard the sounds of three shots. My thoughts were still in the 19th century. Were these the signals given by Oman Arabs to with pull up the draw bridge? Shadows continued their dances. I also desired to dance along with these shapes – only if I could get hold of a black burqua!

Suddenly someone gave me a sharp slap on my cheek. A black shape! I jumped up. That coldness of the slap seemed to have wakened me up. My brain, which had tightened to the point of breaking up soon, seemed to loosen itself.

Some commotions were taking place in the fort. Without taking into account these developments the clock tower struck eleven. The booms of the tower clock seemed to caress my senses slowly. I seemed to regain consciousness.

I could hear the urgent summons of my heart beat "run, run!" I ran, making my way between the shadows. I ran through the way right in front of me, caring not to where! Racing down the narrow path, I finally reached the broad beach again. Ba'o bab trees with bulging trunks stood as sentries there. The sea with its grey color, the rafts with their sails taken down and tied securely – all seemed to create an image of a huge forest.

I don't know how far or how long I ran through the beach. Seeing street lights a little further away, I turned towards them. I realized that I have reached the street corner near my Malayali host Shri Kurup's house. I could recognize the burnt frame of a house which I had noted as a mark to find the way back to Kurup's house. Kurup was waiting anxiously in front of his house. He was worried where I had gone.

He sighed with obvious pleasure that I was safe. Then he looked over me suspiciously and asked "did you go swimming in the sea? You seem wet?" Yes! Wet I was, from sweating! "I had walked in a hurry. That is why I am sweating" I managed to mumble a reply.

"Then where were you for such a long time? I had wanted to tell you before you go out that you should restrict your walking to this street. Murderous gangs are on the increase in Mombasa now. In the Southern part of the city curfew is in force after 8.00 pm. I was afraid whether you had gone to that side. Where have you been?" he asked, in all anxiety.

I suddenly invented a blatant lie. "I had gone to a nearby park. I slept away because of the sea breeze!"

"You should not have done that. There are a number of burqua clad beauties who try to attract strangers. Good luck that you escaped without any danger. From now on do not go out after dusk, OK?" said Kurup, leading me into the spacious hall of his house. I tried to smile; but I knew only too well that it was a failure. Kurup must have felt that something had happened to me. He said in a kind voice " have a good bathe in cold water!" I poured cup after cup of cold water over my head. What Kurup had said was correct. I felt slightly better. I went to bed early after having just one cup of hot coffee.

I woke up the next morning with severe illness. Touching my forehead, Kurup said that this was the onset of malaria. No one can go away from Africa without being affected by malaria at least once. He promised to send a doctor to treat me. The doctor came, concurred with Kurup's diagnosis and gave me injections and a set of yellow tablets.

When Kurup returned from his office that evening he had in his hand a copy of Mombasa Times, an evening paper. He went for a bath leaving the English paper on my bed. I leafed through it. One front page news item caught my attention. It read thus:

Head of secret gang dies in police shoot out

Mombasa,

September 15

The leader of the notorious Hamdara secret gang, One eyed Hasan was killed around 11.00 pm last night by police near Jesus Fort. His friend and security guard Yoosuf, who had been injured in the shootout, has been arrested.

Enough evidence has been collected to prove that many of the killings that took place in and around Mombasa in the past few months have been handiwork of the Hamdara gang. The special anti crime squad, formed by the government under the leadership of Capt Kole had been working on the gang for the past three months.

The squad members had followed one person, who was suspected to have been a member of the gang to Jesus fort. On their signal, two vans full of armed police rushed to the Southern part of the fort. The squad had been equipped with all modern facilities like radio, search lights etc. The attack was mounted suddenly, without any notice.In spite of that most of the gang members were able to escape. However the police managed to shoot down two members; one was the chief of the gang One eyed Hasan and the other was his right hand man Yoosuf.

It is to be noted that One eyed Hasan had escaped four months ago from the jail in Jesus Fort after having been jailed on a murder case.

The Hamdara gang specializes in roaming around the city in black burquas. They do not use weapons. Their specialty is to kill people by wringing their necks.

On one side of the story a photo of Hasan had also been published, I stared at it. The one eye seemed to be glowing. In the green light of that eye I could see a whole world of stories waiting to be told. The centre piece of those stories were a black woman gone mad with love and a Portugese soldier gone mad with jewels!

The caption of the photo read "Mankiller Hasan"; I corrected it using my green ink pen as "Story Teller Hasan"!

THE END

9 788188 025596

Printed by Libri Plureos GmbH in Hamburg,
Germany